Lily's Treasure Map

Kristina Lambert

INFOMAX
COMMON CORE
READERS

Rosen
Classroom™

New York

Published in 2013 by The Rosen Publishing Group, Inc.
29 East 21st Street, New York, NY 10010

Book Design: Michael Harmon

Photo Credits: Cover Ryan McVay/Photodisc/Getty Images; p. 4 Ryan McVay/Thinkstock.com; p. 6 Rob Marmion/
Shutterstock.com; p. 7 Jupiterimages/Thinkstock.com; pp. 9, 11, 19 iStockphoto/Thinkstock.com; p. 12 Brand X
Pictures/Thinkstock.com; p. 14 MGP/Taxi/Getty Images; p. 15 Zooner/Thinkstock.com; p. 17 Medioimages/Photodisc/
Thinkstock.com; p. 20 Hemera/Thinkstock.com; p. 21 Banana Stock/Thinkstock.com.

ISBN: 978-1-4488-8998-3
6-pack ISBN: 978-1-4488-8999-0

Manufactured in the United States of America

CPSIA Compliance Information: Batch #WS12RC: For further information contact Rosen Publishing, New York, New York at 1-800-237-9932.

Word Count: 340

Contents

A Treasure Hunt

Lily wants to find a **treasure**.

A treasure is a kind of prize!

Treasures are often hidden in special places.

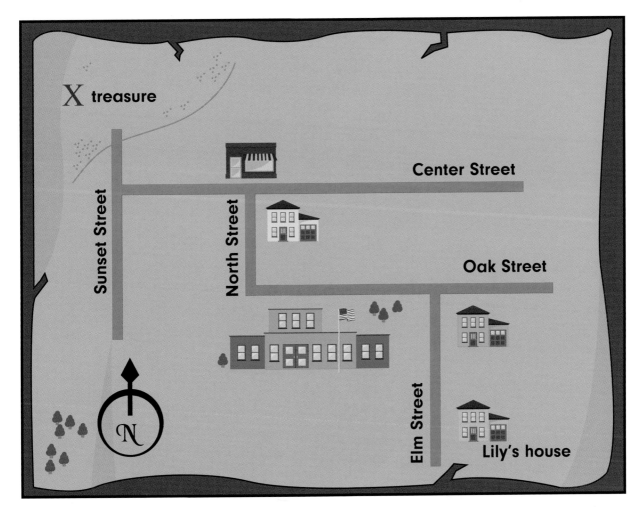

Lily has a treasure map.

Her grandma gave it to her.

It shows her where the treasure is.

Lily starts her treasure hunt at her house.

Who helps Lily find the treasure?

Her grandpa helps her.

He helps her read the map.

On Lily's Street

Lily and her grandpa walk down her street.

She lives on Elm Street.

Lily sees her **neighbor** Alex.

Oak Street

What street should Lily and her grandpa go on next?

The map says they should go on Oak Street.

They make a left turn onto Oak Street.

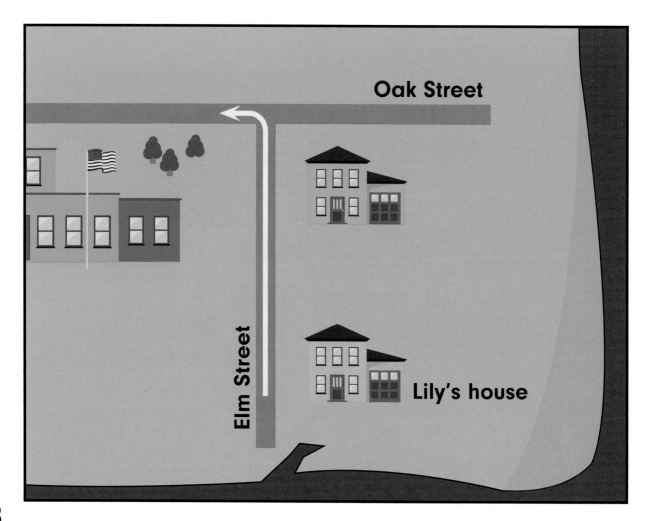

What building do Lily and her grandpa pass

on Oak Street?

They pass Lily's school.

It's a big school!

North Street

Lily and her grandpa make a right turn after they go by Lily's school.

They turn onto North Street.

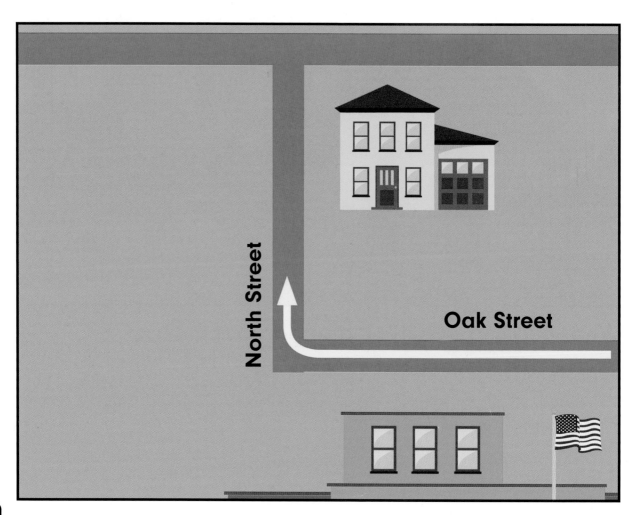

Who lives on North Street?

Lily's Aunt Sarah lives on North Street.

Lily sees Aunt Sarah's dog.

His name is Max.

Center Street

What does Lily see at the end of North Street?

She sees Center Street.

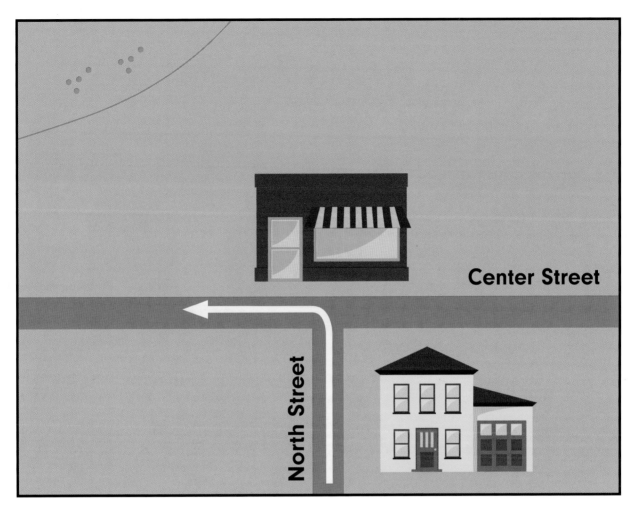

Which way should Lily and her grandpa turn

onto Center Street?

They should turn left.

What store is on Center Street?

The toy store is on Center Street.

Lily and her grandpa go into the store.

What do Lily and her grandpa buy at the toy store?

They buy a shovel.

They're going to use it to dig for the treasure!

Sunset Street

Where should Lily and her grandpa go next?

They should make a right turn onto Sunset Street.

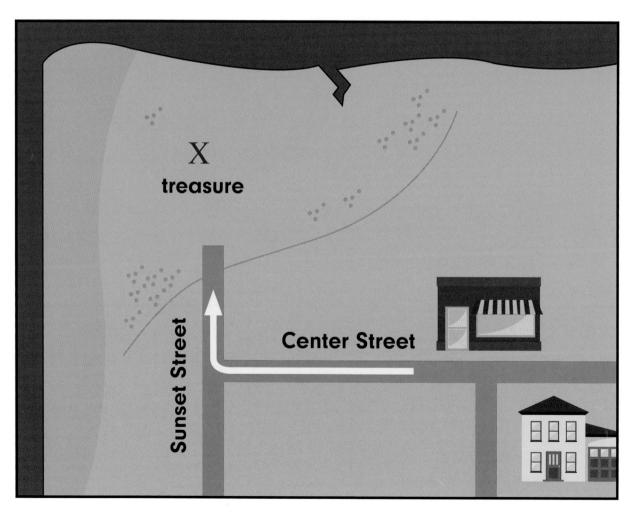

At the Beach

The beach is at the end of Sunset Street!

Lily sees the sand and the water.

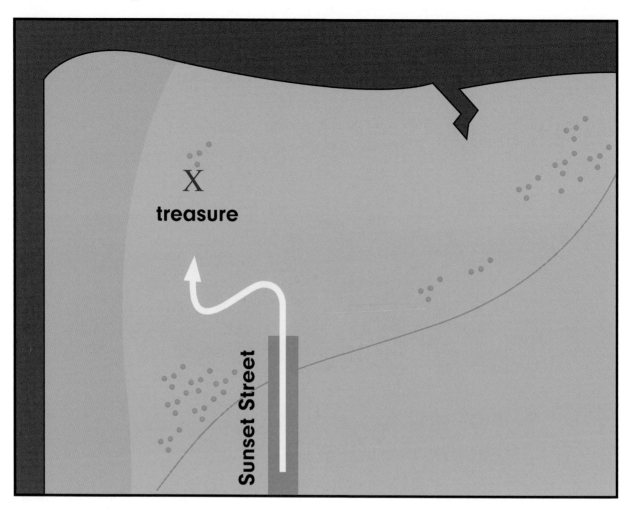

Lily and her grandpa walk toward the treasure.

They walk in the sand.

Digging for Treasure

Lily sees her grandma at the beach!

She tells Lily where her treasure is hidden.

Then, Lily digs for it with her new shovel.

What is Lily's treasure?

It's new toys to play with at the beach!

Lily had fun looking for her treasure!

What kind of treasure would you like to find?

Find the Treasure!

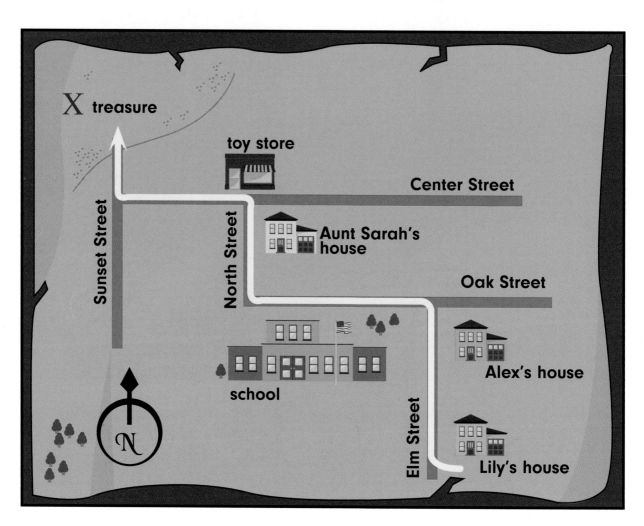

Glossary

neighbor (NAY-buhr) Someone who lives near you.

treasure (TREH-zhuhr) A prize or riches.

Index